Our darling Stella was born six weeks premature. She spent 16 days in NICU. She is so healthy and strong now, we wonder how we ever questioned her resolve. She is a blessing every day and we love her so much. This book is dedicated to Stella Bea.

www.mascotbooks.com

Is There Anything More This Day is Good For?

For more information, please contact:
Mascot Books
620 Herndon Parkway, Suite 320
Herndon, VA 20170
info@mascotbooks.com

Library of Congress Control Number: 2019908904

CPSIA Code: PRT1219A
ISBN-13: 978-1-64307-556-3

Printed in the United States

Is There Anything More This Day is Good For?

(a poem from dad to baby)

written by **Brandon Potter**

illustrated by Sabine Sütterlin Hutto

I walk through the door and I wonder once more,

What to do with this day's remains.

The clock on the wall says not much time at all

As the whole of this day quickly wanes.

Is there anything more this day is good for?

It started like any other day.

We woke up, got dressed, and then surely got stressed

About something that got in our way.

Is there anything more this day is good for?

I feel like the answer is no.

I was in a hurry, the whole day seems blurry,

Maybe tomorrow will be a better go.

There is nothing more this day is good for,

We've worked and played this day away.

The bright yellow sun's chores are all done;

The moon and stars now light our way.

There is nothing more this day is good for,

Time seems to fly when things are fun.

When things get tough though, the slower time goes,

A day, you see, is lost or won.

There is nothing more this day is good for

Than to count our blessings and rest.

The more slumber we get, the less we must fret

About tomorrow's unknown requests.

There must be more this day is good for,

Precious memories to conclude our days.

And now I can see, as you look up at me,

The folly realized in my ways.

I'm thinking of more to use this day for,

We've not even a second to squander.

My love for you, and your mommy too,

Is why I lie awake and I ponder.

And lastly my dear, if you'll lend me your ear,

I realize now something's quite true.

There is something more this day is good for:

To tell you goodnight and I love you.

Stella Bea

A Note from the Author

I wrote this poem as a reminder to myself that even though some days it seems I only have a few minutes with my daughter Stella, it's so important to make the best of them.

One night before bedtime and after a really busy day during a really busy week of a really busy month, I said to myself, "There is nothing more this day is good for." I said it with hopes it would help me fall asleep, but it had the opposite effect. I immediately sat up in bed and wrote this poem. It just flowed out of me. I had to share the message that there is always more a day is good for.

About the Author

Brandon Potter is a photographer, graphic artist, and screen printer from Kinston, North Carolina. Since his youth, he has felt the need to express himself through the use of art and storytelling. His new role as a father has seemed to open his emotional floodgates, inspiring him to try his hand at writing. He also hopes that his heartfelt sentiments will resonate with other parents. Surely the first of many works inspired by his daughter, Stella, Brandon hopes this book will help you take an extra moment with your son or daughter and let them know just how special they are.